The STAR FESTIVAL

MONI RITCHIE HADLEY   ILLUSTRATED BY MIZUHO FUJISAWA

ALBERT WHITMAN & COMPANY
CHICAGO, ILLINOIS

Keiko shouts so all of Japan can hear. "Today is the Tanabata Matsuri!"
It is her fifth Star Festival. It is Oba's eighty-fifth.

Mama hushes Keiko.

But Keiko and Oba scream together. "TANABATA MATSURI!"

Keiko ties a paper wish to a branch of a bamboo tree. "Oba, what is your tanzaku this year?"

"My wish is to eat shaved ice!" Oba says. They share a toothless giggle.

Keiko slips on her summer kimono.
She watches Oba fold the right side first, then the left.

"Do you remember the story of Tanabata?" Oba asks.

"No." Keiko wraps the obi round and around her waist.

Mama reties it.

"One star, Hikoboshi, fell in love with another star, Orihime, who lived at the far end of the sky. He was a cowherd and she was a weaver. When they married, they neglected their work."

"I always do my chores." Keiko smiles proudly at Oba.

"Yes, Keiko-chan. How nicely you have decorated the futon with your pajamas!" Mama picks up, and Keiko follows.

"Orihime's father, the Emperor of the Heavens, forbade her from seeing Hikoboshi—except for once a year, after they fulfilled their duties."

"How mean!" Keiko puts on her geta.

Oops.

"The first time they tried to meet,
Orihime and Hikoboshi could not cross
the Milky Way, the heavenly river dividing
the skies. So a flock of magpies made a bridge
with their wings and reunited them."

"If I were them, I would SWIM across the river," Keiko says.

Finally ready, Keiko and Oba trail behind Mama through town,
over the bridge, up, up, down, down, and into the sea of celebration.

"Stay close," Mama says.

"Okay!" Keiko runs through colorful streamers hanging from the sky.

Mama chases her. Oba follows.
They find Keiko at the game booth scooping goldfish.

Mama says, "Only one."

Oba slips Keiko another coin with a wink.

"I'm hungry! Let's get nagashi somen." Keiko finds a seat at a table with a long bamboo chute. She plunges her chopsticks into the flowing noodles. "Got it!"

Mama catches up with her.

"It's delicious, Mama. The icy noodles slip right into my tummy."

Mama sits down and grabs a seat for Oba.

"Oba? Where is Oba?" Mama scans the crowd and grabs Keiko's hand.

Keiko struggles to keep up with Mama. *Click, click, click.* Her geta bat the pavement.

"Oba, Oba!"

Keiko and Mama are sandwiched in the crowd and cannot move.

"Mama, we are stuck in Hikoboshi's herd. Moooooo!"

Mama and Keiko run to the beat of drums.

BOOM. BOOM. BOOM.

A drop hits Keiko's nose, then pouring rain. She lets it wash her face. "Mama, Orihime's tears are falling from the sky."

Mama rests, breathing in, out, in, out. "How will we find Oba?"

"Lift me higher." Keiko climbs onto Mama's shoulders. "Whoooaaa."

"Do you see her?"

Keiko scans the crowd. Obaasans in kimonos look alike, but Keiko can spot Oba anywhere. "Over there!"

A parade of dancers and taiko drummers surge like a river, separating her from Keiko and Mama.

Keiko scrambles down. "Mama, we need to SWIM across the Milky Way to get to Oba!"

"We cannot run through the performance, Keiko."

Keiko watches the banging bachi. They swing left and right, the movement unrelenting. Then the booming stops, and the dancers bow.

"Now!" Keiko dives in.

Mama follows.

They swim through bachi, fans, arms, rain, and dripping
wet streamers.

They reach the other side. Vendors sell savory pancakes,
meat on sticks, and...

shaved ice.

Keiko runs to Oba and hugs her legs.
"The stars helped us find you, Oba."

"And look who helped me,
the Emperor of the Heavens."
Oba thanks the security guard.

Just as the rain slows to a stop, the skies explode.

"Hikoboshi and Orihime found each other!" Keiko says.

When they return home, Keiko, Oba, and Mama burn their tanzaku.

"Now my wish will come true. What was your tanzaku, Mama?" asks Keiko.

"Exercise!" She giggles.

"And yours?" Oba asks Keiko.

"Shaved ice!"

TANABATA MATSURI

The Japanese Tanabata Festival celebrates the reunion of the mythological lovers Orihime and Hikoboshi, who were separated by the Emperor of the Heavens for neglecting their work when they married. They are represented by the stars Vega and Altair, which is why the celebration is also called the Star Festival. The festival is rooted in the Chinese Qixi holiday, Chinese Valentine's Day, and was brought to Japan in 755 CE by the Empress Kōken.

While the story of Orihime and Hikoboshi varies in its telling, it is said that the two lovers must wait until the following year to reunite if it rains. The people of Japan wish for clear skies on the day of the festival so that the magpies can build a bridge of wings across the Milky Way to reunite them.

The festival became popular in the early seventeenth century. Its traditions are influenced by other Japanese festivals occurring at the same time of year. The Bon Odori, a folk dance, is borrowed from the Obon Festival, which honors the spirits of ancestors. More than two million people attend the Tanabata Matsuri each year. They dance, eat, play games, and gaze at fireworks and towns adorned with color. The largest festivals take place in the Sendai and Hiratsuka regions of Japan.

FOOD

Noodles, representing the threads Orihime weaves, are a popular food item at the matsuri. In some areas of Japan, a long bamboo chute is set up. Cold, flowing noodles, known as nagashi somen, are released into the river chute, scooped up with chopsticks, and dipped into a sauce before eating. Other common festival foods include yakisoba (fried noodles), takoyaki (fried dough balls with octopus), okonomiyaki (grilled pancakes), and yakitori (grilled meat on skewers).

DECORATIONS

Vibrant streamers, representing the weaver's threads, enliven streets, businesses, homes, and train stations. People hang tanzaku, or paper wishes, on bamboo trees, hoping for good luck passing exams, good health, wealth, safety, and, as in Orihime's case, love.

It is believed that the wishes come true when the paper wishes are burned. According to some older traditions, the paper wishes come true when released into the river.

HOW TO MAKE A TANZAKU

1. Cut a bright piece of paper 3 × 6 inches.
2. Punch a hole near the top.
3. Write your wish as the Japanese do: begin at the top right, moving the letters down vertically, then move to the left for your next line.
4. Tie a long, colorful string to the wish, and hang it on the branch of a tree.